there's a **Zombie** in the basement

Written & Illustrated by Stan Yan

For Ava— NEVER FEAR!

Stan Yan '18

This book belongs to:_____

SECOND EDITION

Printed in the United States

Library of Congress Control Number: 2016901892

CPSIA Code: PRT0617B

ISBN-13: 978-0-9755041-3-0
ISBN-10: 0-9755041-3-4

www.squidworkscomics.com
www.mascotbooks.com
www.theresazombieinthebasement.com

For Milo,
for being afraid of my zombie artwork,
which inspired me to write this story.

Mommy! Daddy! I need you please!

A vampire is laughing!
They dance on the stairs!

They'll use safety scissors
and cut off my hair!

You're just being silly. You know it's not true.
Your scissors are sitting right next to your glue.

Now get back to sleep,
I'll tuck you right in.

Our patience with you
is wearing quite thin.

Or maybe Sasquatch
will sit on my head!

Or juggling sharks,
or evil twins.

The nape of my neck
feels needles and pins.

Yes! That's what I fear,
is coming this time!

A zombie, Sasquatch and even a mime!

The centaur is friends with
the pink colored pony!

They all need a friend.
Sometimes they get lonely.

The juggling sharks and
the twins are just sad.

The zombie's their mom.
The vampire's their dad.

They went to the circus to watch Lady Spider
on the trapeze and drink Alien's cider.

All those things you hear are no longer so creepy.

Their party's ending, everyone's getting sleepy.

Now doze off, no counting,
    not even a peep.

Reaper and ghost will take care of your sheep.

All things that you fear,
can really be friends,

'cause it's all what you make
in your mind at the end.

What are you scared of?

Draw a picture of it here!

What others are saying about this book:

Denver-based zombie caricature artist, *Stan Yan* writes and illustrates comic books and graphic novels, teaches and enjoys doing school readings and monster drawing workshops.

stanyan.me